The Dare

Story by Tania Cox

Illustrations by Claudia Vlakancic

The Dare

Text: Tania Cox
Publishers: Tania Mazzeo and Eliza Webb
Series consultant: Amanda Sutera
Hands on Heads Consulting
Editor: Jess Mackay
Project editor: Annabel Smith
Designer: Jess Kelly
Project designer: Danielle Maccarone
Illustrations: Claudia Vlakancic
Production controller: Renee Tome

NovaStar

ISBN 978 0 17 033515 7

Cengage Learning Australia
Level 5, 80 Dorcas Street
Southbank VIC 3006 Australia
Phone: 1300 790 853
Email: aust.nelsonprimary@cengage.com

For learning solutions, visit **cengage.com.au**

Printed in China by 1010 Printing International Ltd
1 2 3 4 5 6 7 29 28 27 26 25

Nelson acknowledges the Traditional Owners and Custodians of the lands of all First Nations Peoples. We pay respect to Elders past and present, and extend that respect to all First Nations Peoples today.

Contents

Chapter 1

The Cottage

"I'm telling you, it's true," blurted Phoebe, Ava's friend, as soon as she arrived for a sleepover. "That cottage is haunted." She pointed a trembling finger to the white, wooden cottage in the backyard of the house where Ava was staying for the summer holidays.

Ava laughed. "Calm down, Phoebe. That cottage is as haunted as your backpack. My Nonna and Nonno Pelusi lived there fifty years ago when they started their restaurant. They never said anything about it being haunted. The only reason they sold the cottage a few years later was to live closer to Pelusi's Pasta Piazza, not because of ghosts."

Phoebe put her backpack down on the cracked, paved path leading to the cottage. "All the kids at school say it, too. Ever since Vanessa moved in next door a couple of months ago, she keeps telling us she's seen shadows creeping around inside the cottage and heard strange noises coming from it."

Ava looked over at Vanessa's sprawling house next door, which took up most of their yard. *I remember Vanessa from school*, she thought.

Ava was born in Prospector Hills and had lived across the road from Phoebe, only a few streets away from the cottage, until she was eight years old. Then Mum got a job as a pharmacist in the city, a whole day's drive away, and they had to leave Prospector Hills. Now, four years later, they were back here for the summer holidays.

Greg, the pharmacist at Lui's Herbal and Traditional Medicine, who Mum was filling in for, was the owner of the cottage. He was letting Mum and Ava stay in the house he had built in front of the cottage.

"Vanessa was telling ghost stories when I was at school with you both," said Ava, rolling her eyes. "Sounds like she's still telling them now at twelve years old! It's probably a big, fat possum running around inside the cottage making shadows and knocking things over."

Phoebe shrugged. "Guess you must be really happy, staying so close to your grandparents' cottage."

Ava nodded. "Being so close to the cottage is like being close to Nonna and Nonno," she said. "The cottage was special to them both. Nonna made her first batch of homemade pasta in there. Nonna and Nonno grew the tomatoes in their garden to use in the pasta sauce. They would always cook heaps of pasta and invite their neighbours over for dinner. The neighbours loved it so much, they begged Nonna and Nonno to open up a restaurant so they could eat it every night! And that's where they got the idea to start their own restaurant."

"Lucky neighbours!" Phoebe laughed. "I would've loved to have been neighbours with your grandparents."

Ava sighed. She and Mum missed Nonna and Nonno so much. They had both passed away shortly before Mum and Ava moved. Ava's aunty had taken over running the restaurant.

"I can't wait to spend lots of time in the cottage, have dinner at Pelusi's Pasta Piazza and eat a burger from Thunderbolt's Tavern. It's my most favourite food after Pelusi's spaghetti bolognaise. My stomach has been rumbling for spaghetti and burgers since we arrived early this morning."

"You should try the new Thunderbolt 1865. It's the best burger! It's named after the year Captain Thunderbolt first came to town," said Phoebe. "But the people in the town nearby where Dad works say that Thunderbolt never came here, and the tavern should change its name. I don't think that's true. I'd love to prove them wrong."

Just then, a car drove into the driveway next door.

Chapter 2

The Dare

A young girl got out of the car and looked over towards Ava and Phoebe. She waved.

"Hi, Phoebe," said Vanessa, walking up to the fence between her house and the cottage. "Hey, Ava! Have you moved back here?"

"Hi, Vanessa," said Ava. She explained to Vanessa why she was here.

"Great!" said Vanessa. "My family's celebrating one hundred years since my great-great-grandfather opened up Lui's Herbal and Traditional Medicine way back in 1924. There's going to be a super sale, a huge celebration cake and loads of cool giveaway prizes! You'll both have to come next week."

"Sounds like fun," said Ava, smiling. Mum had already mentioned it to her.

"Got to go now," said Vanessa. "I'm helping Mum make a photo collage to display at the celebrations next week, but it's really hard to find early photos of the pharmacy. My grandparents' house was flooded before Mum was even born, and all the photos of her family's history were destroyed."

"Hopefully you can find some," replied Ava. "I can't imagine how sad I'd feel if the photos of my family's history were destroyed."

Vanessa turned to leave, and Ava looked at Phoebe with excitement. "Come on! I want to spend some time in the cottage before it gets too dark. The last time I was in it was when Greg invited Mum and me to come and look at the cottage just before we left Prospector Hills. He'd only just bought the place and knew that it had once belonged to Nonna and Nonno."

"Wait!" Vanessa gasped, turning back around. 'You mean *that* cottage?' She pointed dramatically to the old cottage.

"Sure do," said Ava.

"You know it's haunted, right?" whispered Vanessa.

"I did try to tell Ava," said Phoebe, shuddering slightly.

"Yes, Phoebe did mention it like a hundred times," said Ava. "But my nonna and nonno used to live there, so it's special to me. And it's definitely not haunted."

"I suppose it would be special to me, too, if any of my family had lived there years ago," said Vanessa. "But it's so old. And haunted. And since we only have a small backyard, my parents want to buy most of Greg's backyard and the cottage. They want to knock over part of the fence and the cottage to put a pool there. I heard Dad and Greg talking about it yesterday at the pharmacy before Greg left to go on holidays."

"Vanessa, your backyard will be huge! And a pool will be so awesome!" said Phoebe.

Ava's eyes widened. "I didn't know your family wanted to buy the cottage!" she gasped.

Vanessa nodded. "I'll be glad to see that old, haunted dump of a cottage go."

Ava's stomach coiled like a snake. "It's *not* haunted! And it's not a dump either," she snapped. Then she took a deep breath. *I've got to try to save Nonna and Nonno's cottage somehow,* she thought.

"I can't wait to have pool parties. The next time you visit, Ava, you can come over for a swim," said Vanessa. "It should be built by then. You too, Phoebe."

"Cool," said Phoebe.

"No, it's not," cried Ava. "Vanessa, with such a huge yard, there has to be another place to put the pool without knocking down the cottage. Can't you talk to your parents about it, *please*? Just think, if you keep the cottage, you could make it into a really cute sleepover place to have at your pool parties."

"That's a super-fun idea," said Vanessa, her eyes lighting up for a moment and then dimming again. "If the cottage wasn't haunted! No one will want to sleep there."

Then Vanessa seemed to think for a while. "Tell you what, I'll talk to my parents about not knocking down the cottage. There was another spot we sort of talked about putting the pool. That way, the next time you visit, you can come for a pool party in our new pool and a sleepover in the cottage."

Ava let out a huge sigh. "Fantastic! Thanks ..."

"But," continued Vanessa, with a mischievous look in her eyes, "before I talk to Mum and Dad, you have to stay overnight in that cottage. If you can stay in it overnight, that'll mean others can stay in it for sleepovers, too. You can go as well if you want, Phoebe. So, what do you think, Ava? I dare you ..."

Chapter 3

The Decision

For Ava, there was only one answer. "Dare accepted," she said, folding her arms and smiling at Vanessa.

"Really?" Vanessa gasped. "You're going to stay in *there*?" She pointed towards the cottage.

"Really?" Phoebe squeaked. She squatted down to the ground, mumbling something about a shoelace.

"Of course we are," said Ava. "Anything to save Nonna and Nonno's cottage. The place where they made their very first batch of pasta. It was so special to them. Let's get our things together for tonight, Phoebe. See you tomorrow, Vanessa."

Vanessa waved. "Okay, see you tomorrow. I hope."

"Hurry, Phoebe. You're taking ages to tie up one shoelace. Let's go tell Mum about tonight and then pack," said Ava, looking down at Phoebe still crouched on the ground.

"Phoebe? Phoebe!" cried Ava, suddenly noticing Phoebe's pale face. "Are you okay? Are you sick?"

"Yeah," said Phoebe. "I'm scared sick about staying in the cottage tonight. I didn't have a shoelace to tie up. Thought I might faint just at the thought of staying there." She stood up, wonkily. "And I still might."

Ava bit her bottom lip. *I didn't even ask Phoebe what she wanted to do*, she thought. "Phoebe, I'm so sorry," she said. "I should've asked you first if you wanted to come. But I'll be fine to stay there by myself."

Ava looked over at the old cottage. Out-of-control vines crept over it and wood was visible beneath the cracked white paint. The wind was blowing through a slightly open window, making the tattered curtains inside restless. *I sort of understand why Phoebe and Vanessa think it's haunted, or at least looks haunted*, Ava thought.

"Ava, I'm coming with you to save the cottage. Fainting or not," said Phoebe, smiling weakly.

Inside the house, as they packed a few of their things, Mum arrived back from work. Ava told her what Vanessa said about the cottage.

Mum laughed. "That cottage isn't haunted.

And yes, of course you can have a sleepover in there tonight."

"But is it true about the cottage being sold?" asked Ava, crossing her fingers and her toes.

Mum hugged Ava. "Greg feels that the house, the large yard and the cottage are too big for him to look after. He's always so busy with work. So he's discussing the sale of the cottage and most of the yard with Vanessa's family, which would let them extend their backyard and put in a pool. That way, Greg only has this house to look after."

Ava sighed. *Why did what Vanessa said have to be true*, she thought. Then she took a big breath.

"Well, I'm going to try and save Nonna and Nonno's cottage," she said, pulling a torch and a couple of sleeping bags out of the cupboard.

"Me too. Haunted cottage or not," said Phoebe, shuddering.

Chapter 4

The Card Game

After a very early dinner, Ava and Phoebe walked along the path leading to the front door of the cottage. Ava turned the stiff doorknob on the weathered front door.

"It's stuck," Ava said. She tried turning the knob again and pushing the door with her shoulder. "No luck. Let's try the back door." She hurried along the side of the cottage. "I hope that isn't stuck, too."

"I wouldn't mind if it was," mumbled Phoebe.

Ava had barely touched the back door when it creaked wide open. It was dark now. Dust tickled her nose. "A*choo!*"

Phoebe jumped. "Don't do that again! You gave me a fright!"

"Relax, Phoebe. It was a sneeze from all the dust in here," said Ava, as her fingers fumbled on the wall near the door until she found the light switch.

A light flickered on above the kitchen table. Ava looked around. The wooden cupboards were faded and chipped, just like the table and its four chairs.

"This is where Nonna and Nonno cooked their pasta before they started their restaurant," she said. "Come on, let's set up our sleeping bags in the living room."

"Okay," Phoebe squeaked, trembling.

Ava and Phoebe walked along the hallway until they reached a grainy wooden door. Ava turned the brassy doorknob and pushed it open to darkness. She felt around the wall for the light switch again.

"Found it at last!" she said, flicking on a light that dimly lit the living room. Ava cringed. Millimetres away from her fingers was a huge black spider. *I'm glad Mr Hairy Legs wasn't trying to turn on the light at the same time I was,* she thought.

Phoebe shivered and hugged herself. "I think I prefer the light off," she said, looking around.

"It's just old and uncared for," said Ava, as the timber floorboards groaned with each footstep they took in the living room. She looked around. White paint on the walls peeled endlessly. Carefully woven cobwebs clung to the inside corners of a fireplace, where ash was scattered around in the pit from the last fire that would have happened there long ago.

"Hey, Phoebe. What's that on top of the fireplace?" asked Ava, walking over towards the fireplace mantel that was decorated with rosettes. She picked up a box and lifted the lid.

Phoebe peered over her shoulder. "What is it?"

Ava sneezed again. "A dusty packet of cards and a sand timer." She stared at the word on the packet: SAVE. She flipped the packet over. Faded instructions were on the back. "Do you think Nonna and Nonno played this game?"

Phoebe shrugged. "Don't know. Did they have cards back then?"

"Of course they did, Phoebe. They were here fifty years ago, not fifty million years ago." Ava laughed. She began to read the instructions.

"Deal out the cards face down amongst the players. Turn over the sand timer and begin the game. Each player takes turns placing one card face up in the centre of the playing area.

"When two cards match, any player can yell 'SAVE!' and cover the pile with their hand to collect the cards. The game must be played until all the cards have been played, declaring the one with the most cards the winner.

"*But* the game must be finished before the sand timer runs out. Or else the players will have to save themselves ..."

"Sort of sounds like a game of 'Snap'!" said Ava.

"But 'Snap' doesn't have that creepy ending," said Phoebe, squirming. "I wonder what it means?"

Something was written beneath the thick layer of dust on the sand timer. Ava wiped off some of the dust and stifled a sneeze.

"Look what's written on the sand timer." She pointed to the timer and began to read the words. "Yell 'SAVE!' before the sand runs out or save yourself ..."

Phoebe frowned. "It's like what was written in the instructions."

"This card game sounds really cool," said Ava, spreading out her sleeping bag. "We should play it."

Phoebe spread out her sleeping bag and then sat down on it. “I suppose it will get my mind off all the possum noises in here,” she said, half-smiling.

Ava laughed. “That’s right. There are lots of big, fat possum noises in here. Besides, you might enjoy the game, even though I’ll probably win.” She started dealing the cards.

“I wouldn’t be too sure about enjoying the game,” mumbled Phoebe. “But I am pretty sure I’ll win. Let’s start!” She flipped over the sand timer.

They hadn’t been playing long when Ava placed a card down that had a strange picture of a shabby hat with a thick headband above its brim. The word “SAVE” was written beneath it.

“I don’t know why, but that hat looks familiar,” said Phoebe, placing down an identical card on top of it. “Save!” she yelled, slapping her hand down on the cards.

Suddenly, the lights flickered. Then, all was dark ...

Chapter 5

The Oil Lamps

The lights flickered on, but they weren't normal lights.

Ava looked around with her mouth wide open. Oil lamps glowed around the room. "Where are we?" she whispered, her heartbeat sprinting throughout her body.

Phoebe opened her mouth but only a squeak came out. Then she said, "I don't know. But I do know one thing: we aren't in the cottage. I also know that this would be a very suitable time for me to faint."

"Phoebe, this is definitely not a suitable time for you to faint, or even think about fainting."

Ava looked around. She stared at the fireplace, then quickly walked over to it. She picked up an oil lamp and held it up close to the fireplace mantel.

Rosettes? thought Ava.

Her heart skipped a complete beat. Ava spun towards Phoebe.

"Look! We're still in the living room of the cottage. See how the fireplace mantel is decorated with rosettes? Exactly like Nonna and Nonno's. I'll turn on the light so you can have a better look."

"I'm not sure if I want to have a better look," said Phoebe.

That's strange; there's no light switch here, Ava thought. Her heart was now skipping ten complete beats at a time! She walked slowly around the room with the oil lamp.

"The rest of the room sort of seems the same as Nonna and Nonno's cottage," Ava finally said. "It *has* to be the same cottage. Just with older furniture and rugs, like what I see at the antique store when I go there with Mum."

Ava held the oil lamp closer to the wall. "And the walls have flowery wallpaper instead of white paint. I don't know whether to feel excited, scared or both!"

Ava stopped at the window. The sun was just starting to rise. Lots of trees surrounded the cottage, rather than neighbourly houses.

"Well, I'm definitely not excited! I told you this cottage was haunted," said Phoebe, quivering as she looked around. "So is that creepy card game."

Ava looked down at the sand timer and cards. "Phoebe! Look at the cards! The ones with the hats. They're glowing!"

"The words on the sand timer are, too!" Phoebe gasped. "And sand is pouring quickly through it."

Ava took a deep breath and stared at the sand timer. The words "Yell 'SAVE!' before the sand runs out or save yourself" glowed softly.

"Do you think we have to keep playing to finish this game and get out of here?" Ava asked Phoebe in a panic.

"I don't know," Phoebe replied in a small voice, looking even more panicked.

"Come on, Phoebe. Let's at least try," said Ava, sitting down quickly on the rug that now replaced their sleeping bags.

"I want to go home. I don't want to be stuck here having to save myself when the sand timer runs out. I can hardly save myself from my little sister's new, crazy kitten!" said Phoebe, but she sat down, too.

Phoebe reached for a card from her pile to

place down. She seemed to struggle.

"What's wrong?" asked Ava. "We need to hurry up and play."

"Tell these creepy cards that! They're stuck," said Phoebe, frowning.

Ava tried to pick up a card from her pile. "It's like they've been glued together," she said.

Why would they be stuck? Are they trying to keep us here? she thought wildly. Just then, one of the glowing cards with the old hat on it fluttered towards the door. It kept fluttering against it.

"Phoebe! That card!" Ava gulped as fear soared through her body. She pinched herself hard on her leg to make sure she wasn't dreaming. "Are you seeing what I'm seeing?"

Phoebe's eyes bulged. Then she rubbed her eyes and opened them again. "Unfortunately, yes," she said. "It's so, so creepy."

A stampede of elephants filled Ava's stomach. "I think it's trying to tell us something, like it wants us to follow it out the door," she said, standing up on wonky legs. "Come on, Phoebe. Let's go."

Chapter 6

The Hat

"Now I really do want to faint!" whispered Phoebe, grabbing the sand timer and following Ava towards the door.

"Phoebe, we don't have time!" said Ava, pointing to the precious grains tumbling through the sand timer. "Somehow this all feels connected to the game and the timer. We have to hurry. You can faint when we get back home."

"If we ever get back home," muttered Phoebe. "Let's hope whatever this creepy card wants to show us will be quick, because there's no pause button on this sand timer! I'll keep an eye on it and make sure we're not taking too long."

Ava and Phoebe followed the fluttering card back along the hallway until it stopped outside the kitchen door, which was slightly open. Ava picked up the glowing card from the floor.

Just then, loud laughter filled the air.

Ava and Phoebe crouched down. They peered through the opening of the door in the dim morning light. Ava gasped. Phoebe gulped.

Three bearded men in torn, long-sleeve shirts and long trousers were sitting around a small table, laughing. One of the men, who had a thin moustache and was wearing a hat, reached into a black bag.

That hat looks familiar, thought Ava, looking down at the card. Then she realised why. "Phoebe! That's the hat on the card!"

Phoebe's eyes widened as she nodded. "I've seen that hat somewhere else."

The man wearing the hat slowly pulled out some gold chains, sparkly necklaces and rings from the black bag. "What a swag we got ourselves today!" He laughed.

"Thieves?" Ava whispered to Phoebe.

Phoebe instantly turned white.

"Can't wait for the next swag, Captain Thunderbolt!" said one of the other men, rubbing his hands together. They all burst out laughing.

Ava and Phoebe looked at each other with mouths open.

"Bushrangers!" whispered Ava.

"Captain Thunderbolt?" exclaimed Phoebe. "As in the Thunderbolt 1865 burger? Ava! We must be back in the year 1865! They named that burger because it was the year that he first came to the town, remember? And that hat looks exactly like the one he wears in the picture at the Tavern."

Ava almost choked on the tennis-ball-sized lump in her throat. *Captain Thunderbolt was here in Nonna and Nonno's cottage all those years ago?* she thought. So, *if the hat on the card is Captain Thunderbolt's, why did the card lead us here? And what does the word* "SAVE" *have to do with it?*

She looked down at the card. Her eyes widened. "Phoebe, for some reason the hat card has stopped glowing," she whispered.

Phoebe looked at the sand timer. "Well, at least it doesn't mean that we've run out of time."

Ava thought for a moment. "Could it mean that it has showed us what it wanted to? That Captain Thunderbolt was here in the cottage? Do you think there are other glowing cards in the game?" Question after question whizzed around at dizzying speeds in Ava's mind.

Phoebe shrugged. "I just hope there are cards to take us home."

"I think we need to keep playing the game to

find out," said Ava.

Phoebe looked at the sand timer again and nodded quickly. "The sand is running out fast. And the words on it are glowing brighter!" she whispered hoarsely. "I hope the cards aren't still stuck together." As she got up from crouching, she knocked a book off a table.

Ava frowned and put a finger to her lips. She signalled Phoebe to move along the hallway and back to the room where the cards were.

"What was that?" roared Thunderbolt. "I thought you said this place was empty?"

"It is! I went lookin' all over the house after I broke in through the back door," came a reply from one of the men. "Probably the wind."

A chair scraped across the wooden floor. Ava and Phoebe pushed open the living-room door where the cards lay on the rug.

"Please don't be stuck, cards!" begged Phoebe. "I really don't want to meet Captain Thunderbolt right now!" Still clutching the sand timer in one hand, she picked up a card with the other. "Phew! The pile's unstuck at last!" she cried, tossing it down.

It was a card with an unusual picture of a bowl and stick with something engraved at one end of the stick. The word “SAVE” was written underneath the picture.

“Where ya goin’, Thunderbolt?” a voice boomed.

Boots clanked along the hallway. “Goin’ to make sure no one is ’ere.”

“I don’t really want to meet Thunderbolt either!” cried Ava. *Please be a pair! Please! Please! Please!* she thought feverishly.

She didn’t know what was making the most noise: the clanking of the boots getting closer or her heart madly pounding. She grabbed the next card and threw it down. It was the bowl and stick – a pair!

“Save!” Ava yelled, slapping her hand over the cards.

Just then, the door handle clicked.

Suddenly, all went dark.

Chapter 7

The Dragons

When Ava opened her eyes this time, bright sunlight streamed through the windows.

Phoebe still had her eyes squeezed tight. “Please tell me that we’re home *and* in real time.”

Ava looked around, her heart beating fast. The fireplace decorated with rosettes was there. “The room kind of looks the same as the cottage, almost like the time before with Captain Thunderbolt. Yet it’s different,” she said, looking at the faded and torn flowery wallpaper. *Was anyone living here now*? thought Ava. There were cobwebs in every corner.

Phoebe, who had her head buried in her hands, hadn’t looked up yet.

Ava swallowed hard. “Phoebe! Open your eyes! There are ... dragons.”

"Great! First Captain Thunderbolt and now dragons!" blurted Phoebe. Her head sprang up and her eyes flew open. "I really am going to faint!"

Ava shook her head. "I was going to say, there are dragons on a box in the corner of the room near the window!"

Phoebe stood up and stared at the box. "It definitely wasn't in the cottage when we saw Captain Thunderbolt."

Ava wondered what could be inside the box. Holding her breath, she hurried over to the dusty window. Her eyes narrowed as she scanned the neighbourhood. There were more familiar houses nearby now than before when they discovered Captain Thunderbolt in the cottage. *But there are fewer trees around now*, she thought.

"Well," said Ava. "The good news is that this has to be Nonna and Nonno's cottage. But the not-so-good news is that I don't think we're in real time. Yet."

"And the really-not-so-good news is that the timer is now half empty!" said Phoebe, holding it up in the air.

The words "Yell 'SAVE!' before the sand runs out or save yourself" glowed brighter than before.

"Come on, Phoebe. We need to keep playing the game. It must be the only way we can return to real time," said Ava, racing back to the cards.

"Already there," said Phoebe, reaching for a card. "Oh, not again!" Phoebe sighed, shaking her head.

"Is it … Is it stuck?" asked Ava, quietly.

Phoebe nodded. She put her head in her hands.

Just then, Ava saw something move out of the corner of her eye. Something fluttered. Something glowed.

"Look, Phoebe!" said Ava, shaking Phoebe with one hand and pointing to the door. "The card showing the bowl and stick is glowing! And fluttering towards the door. We need to follow it!"

"Do we have to?" asked Phoebe, hugging herself tightly. "I'm not sure I want to find out who it's going to lead us to this time."

Ava stared at her. "Do you want to go back home?"

Phoebe grabbed the sand timer. "Let's go and hope that whatever this card wants to show us won't take long. Or be too scary!"

Chapter 8

The Bowl and the Stick

Ava and Phoebe quietly followed the fluttering card down the hallway again, towards the kitchen.

The card stopped outside the kitchen door that was ajar.

Ava crouched down and tried to look into the room, but the door wasn't quite open enough for her to see anything. She opened it a smidgen more. Then she signalled to Phoebe to crouch down and look inside the kitchen, too.

"Check it out," whispered Phoebe. "What sort of cooking is going on in there?"

Ava gulped. On a small wooden table with two chairs at either side of it sat some small glass jars filled with what looked like dried leaves and powders.

A few twigs and plant roots with branches, some leafy and some not, were laid out on the table, too. On the kitchen bench in one corner was a book with unusual symbols on its cover.

"Chinese writing," Ava whispered. "We're learning Chinese at school."

Next to the book was a small bowl and stick, like the picture on the card. More dragon boxes had appeared everywhere. There was a whole pile of them stacked on top of each other in a corner.

"We need to find out what's happening in there in a hurry, because this sand isn't slowing down," said Phoebe. She held up the sand timer.

The words are glowing brighter than before, thought Ava, frowning. Just then, she saw something move through the kitchen window. A short, thin man with a long beard was gathering plants from small pots outside in the yard.

"Hello, Mr Lui. Have you moved in here?" asked a lady from over the fence.

The man shook his head. "No, I'm only staying here one week. I'm moving into the back of my herbal medicine shop when it opens next week."

"Phoebe!" whispered Ava, straining her neck

to get a better look through the small opening of the door. "I thought I heard that lady call him Mr Lui."

"So did I!" said Phoebe. "But isn't that Vanessa's family name, too?"

Ava's eyes widened so much they felt as if they would pop. "Yes, it is! Do you think this is Mr Lui, as in Vanessa's great-great-grandfather?"

"Could be," said Phoebe. "That man did say something about his herbal medicine shop."

The lady strolled off and the man started walking towards the house.

"Crouch down as much as you can, Phoebe," whispered Ava.

The man entered the kitchen and washed the plants in the sink and then spread them out on a rack.

He opened one of the jars, took out some dried leaves and placed them in the small bowl. Then he seemed to grind them with the stick, making a clicking noise.

"Phoebe, he's using a bowl and stick just like the one in the picture on the card," said Ava.

She squinted slightly and held the card closer. She could just read the small, engraved letters on the stick: LUI. *Lui?* she thought. *That was it!*

It has to be Mr Lui! Vanessa had said that Mr Lui started Lui's Herb and Traditional Medicine back in 1924. She pointed to the stick on the card and showed Phoebe.

"Yes! It definitely has to be Vanessa's great-great-grandfather," whispered Phoebe. "But Vanessa mustn't know he lived in the cottage. Even if it was just for one week. Her family mustn't know either."

Ava thought for a while. "Remember when Vanessa said most of her mum's family photos were destroyed in a flood before her mum was born? I guess some of their history got lost, too."

Phoebe nodded. "I guess so."

Just then, a thought raced across Ava's mind, making goosebumps tickle the tops of her arms. She stared at the word "SAVE".

"What if I could somehow show Vanessa that her great-great-grandfather lived in the same cottage as Nonna and Nonno?" she said. "I doubt Vanessa would want to knock over the cottage, even if Mr Lui only stayed here for a week. We'd be able to *save* the cottage, just like the name of the card game!" She hugged the card.

Phoebe's eyes suddenly lit up. "And Captain Thunderbolt was in this cottage, too! Another good reason to save the cottage, like the game says. It's part of the town's history! We just need to prove it to the nearby town now," said Phoebe.

"I can't wait to finish this game and get home to tell Vanessa!" said Ava, looking down at the card again. "Phoebe, it's stopped glowing like the hat card did last time. It must have shown us what it wanted to: that Vanessa's great-great-grandfather lived here."

Phoebe pointed to the sand timer. "There's more sand at the bottom now than at the top. I'm shaking just thinking about what happens if the sand runs out before we finish the game. What would we do then, Ava? How are we going to save ourselves? What if we *never* get home?"

Ava's heart started to sink as Phoebe spoke. She bit her bottom lip. Then she shook her head and took a deep breath. "Phoebe," she said, "what if we *do* finish the game before the sand runs out? Come on. Let's not waste another single grain of sand worrying about if we don't finish! We've already wasted enough time."

"You're right," said Phoebe, tiptoeing along the hallway past Ava.

By the time Ava got back to the living room, Phoebe was already reaching for the pile of cards.

"Please be unstuck!" whispered Ava, sitting down near Phoebe.

"Please be unstuck *and* take us back home!" begged Phoebe, grabbing a card and tossing it down. "Yes to it being unstuck!"

Another strange picture stared up at them. It was a small, silver machine with the word "SAVE" underneath.

Ava reached quickly for a card. She held her breath and threw down the card. It was a pair. "Save!" yelled Ava, slapping her hand down on the pile. "Please take us home!"

And suddenly, once again, all went dark.

Chapter 9

The Gondola

"Please, please," begged Phoebe, her eyes squeezed tight again. "Let us be home in real time."

Ava took a deep breath as her eyes searched feverishly around the room. The fireplace with its rosettes was still right there in front of her. "Well, at least we're still in Nonna and Nonno's cottage," she said, sighing and looking around.

Swirly wallpaper now covered most of the walls. But on the wall near the window was a bucket of paint and a brush. Some of the wall was stripped of wallpaper and it seemed as though someone had started to paint the wall white.

Ava walked towards the window. Outside, there were even more familiar houses in the street. *But not as many as in real time*, she thought.

"Ava, the suspense is killing me!" said Phoebe, standing up with her eyes still closed. "Are we in real time?"

"I don't think we're quite there yet," said Ava, finally answering her.

"What do you mean?" asked Phoebe, her eyes flying open. She put the sand timer down on the rug. "I'm sick of playing this silly game. I want to go home now! I thought I was coming for a sleepover and a movie night. Not being trapped in some haunted cottage and feeling like we're actually starring in a horror movie ourselves. I just want to go home!"

"And do you think I don't?" snapped Ava. She took another deep breath. Then she looked at the timer. "Phoebe, we don't have time to argue. Check it out for yourself," said Ava. "Three quarters of the sand is at the bottom!"

The words "Yell 'SAVE' before the sand runs out or save yourself" glowed brighter than ever before.

Phoebe stared at the timer and quickly got up. "Definitely a good enough reason to stop arguing!"

Ava pointed to the glowing card that was already fluttering towards the door. "It knows that time is really running out now!" she said.

Phoebe followed the card. “Let’s go! We won’t waste time we don’t have trying to pick up a card. They’ll be stuck together like glue until the card stops glowing.”

Ava opened the door to the hallway. On the shelf was a wooden sculpture of a long, narrow boat with a curved front and back. A man stood at one end, holding a tall, skinny stick.

“That’s a gondola, like the ones in Venice,” whispered Phoebe, as they tiptoed quickly along the hallway. “My mum’s dream holiday place.”

“I know,” said Ava. “There’s a photo of Nonna and Nonno in a gondola when they were young in their restaurant. They were both born in Venice.”

The card fluttered along the hallway again towards the kitchen door, then lay flat on the floor and glowed. But this time, the door was closed. Ava stared at the door.

“This door is different,” she whispered.

Phoebe put her hand on the doorknob.

“Don’t try to open it,” whispered Ava. “For some reason, the door isn’t open this time. Maybe the game didn’t want it to be opened.”

Ava picked up the glowing card. Then she stood on her tiptoes and peered through the small, square glass window.

Chapter 10

The Small, Silver Machine

A petite, dark-haired woman was turning the handle of a small, silver machine that was clamped to the edge of the kitchen table. Her curly, shoulder-length hair fell over the side of her face, making it hard for Ava to see her. As the woman turned the handle, long, stringy strands of pasta came out of the machine.

Pasta? thought Ava. *Sort of how the big automatic machine makes it at Pelusi's.*

The woman placed the long pasta strands on tea towels on the kitchen table. Ava picked up the glowing card. It showed the same machine in the picture on the card. She pointed it out to Phoebe.

Phoebe looked through the glass window. "Hey, I think I see a man in the garden."

Ava looked through the small window in the door again. There was a loud thump at the door that led out to the backyard. "Newspaper, Mr Pelusi!" someone shouted.

"*Grazie!*" replied a young man, waving.

Ava's eyes widened. "Phoebe! Did you hear that?"

Phoebe's mouth was gaping. "Mr Pelusi? Is that your ..."

Ava smiled delightedly. She blinked away tears. "My nonno! And that lady has to be my nonna! We must be in the cottage about fifty years ago."

Just then, the woman moved around the table to spread out more cut pasta.

"Yes!" said Ava. "That's Nonna! I recognise her now from all the photos Mum has shown me!"

Ava looked at the card still glowing in her hand. She hugged it. *Don't worry, Nonna and Nonno. I won't let anyone knock over this cottage,* she thought. *Especially now that I've actually seen you here.*

Ava and Phoebe stood on their tiptoes, looking through the window in the door.

Nonno, carrying an armful of tomatoes and the newspaper, walked in from the backyard.

"Mum always tells me stories about how Nonna and Nonno grew their own tomatoes for the pasta sauce in the restaurant," whispered Ava. "Until the business became so busy that they couldn't grow enough tomatoes to keep up with all the meals being ordered. So trucks started delivering tomatoes and other vegetables to the restaurant. Nonna's recipe for her home-made pasta is still being used in the restaurant today."

Ava took a big breath. "I'm going to say hello to them, Phoebe." She put her hand on the doorknob. "I want to give them a big hug."

"Wait!" said Phoebe. "We aren't in real time. Think about it. They aren't grandparents yet. They're not even parents. How would you explain who you are to them? They would probably faint! Could that be the reason why the door wasn't opened for us this time? The game didn't want you racing up to your grandparents and maybe delaying things for us to get back. Or worse, stopping us!"

Ava thought for a moment. Then she sighed and bit back tears. She wanted so much to hug them.

"You're right." She looked down at the card in her hand. It glowed softer and softer until it stopped. "The card has stopped glowing, Phoebe. It must have shown us all that it wanted to. After seeing Nonna and Nonno here in the cottage, it's made me all the more determined to save it," said Ava. "We'd better get back and find the cards that will take us home."

"Let's find them in a hurry!" said Phoebe. "We can't have much time left now!"

Ava took one last look at Nonna and Nonno, then turned around. But something was wrong. Something was horribly wrong, and missing. Ava's stomach dropped to her toes as she stared at Phoebe's hands. "Phoebe, where's the sand timer?"

Phoebe was already frantically looking around. "I don't know. Did you take it?"

Panic spread through Ava like a bushfire. She looked up and down the hallway, but the sand timer wasn't there.

"No, I didn't. You were the one clinging to it like a teddy bear!"

Phoebe froze, then turned whiter than white. "Ava, do you think we've run out of time?"

"Don't say that," Ava gasped. Her stomach was bouncing up and down like a basketball all the way to her toes. Just then, an idea flashed through her mind. "Let's check the living room. Quick! It's our only hope."

Ava blew a kiss through the window to Nonna and Nonno. As much as she loved them and missed them, she wanted to get back to her mum in real time!

They raced back to the room.

Ava threw open the door. A bright, almost blinding, light filled the room.

"Aaargh! What is that?" cried Phoebe, holding her hand up to her face.

Shielding her face with her hands, Ava peeked through her fingers to search the room. And then she saw it!

"Look! The sand timer! That blazing light is coming from the sand timer," cried Ava.

The words "Yell 'SAVE' before the sand runs out or save yourself" glowed boldly.

"I think there are only a few grains left!" screamed Phoebe, still covering her eyes. "Quick!"

Ava raced helter-skelter to the rug, where there lay only two cards. She threw down a card with a picture of a small cottage and the word "SAVE" written beneath it.

“I can’t stand this light any more!” Phoebe cried, squeezing her eyes shut.

“There are three grains of sand left!” cried Ava, throwing down the last card. It was a match! “Save! Save the cottage!” she shouted. Her hand came crashing down on the card as the last grain of sand fell.

A spectacular golden light filled the entire room.

Then, once again, all went dark.

Chapter 11

Proof from the Past

Ava held her breath as she stared at the rosette fireplace. *That's a good start*, she thought, letting out a long, deep breath. Even the peeling walls were a welcome sight. Ava could feel something soft, smooth and warm under her legs as she sat on the floor. Her sleeping bag!

A *super-good start!* she thought. *But I want to make sure we are back in real time before I say anything to Phoebe.* She could hear a ball bouncing outside. She got up and walked towards the window, holding up her hand to shield her eyes against the bright morning sun.

"Ava!" said Phoebe, sitting down with her eyes

closed. "Are you still there? Say something! I'm almost too scared to ask, but are we home?"

"Just checking that we are," said Ava, as calmly as she possibly could. *I don't want to give Phoebe any false hopes in case we aren't*, she thought, squinting against the sunlight.

Just then, her breathing stopped. She saw who was bouncing the ball. Vanessa was playing basketball in her backyard with her younger brother, Hayden! Ava's heart galloped around her body. She let out a big breath, as if she'd been holding it for days.

"Phoebe! We're ..." But then she froze. She saw something in the corner near the fireplace that didn't belong there. Or did it?

"Phoebe! Quick! Look in the corner near the fireplace!" she blurted, pointing frantically.

"This is not sounding good," cried Phoebe, opening her eyes. She stifled a scream. "Is that what I think it is?"

Ava nodded. "Thunderbolt's hat, Mr Lui's mixing bowl and stick, and Nonna and Nonno's pasta machine. Can you believe it?"

Phoebe seemed to open her mouth to say something, but instead she fell backwards.

"Phoebe!" cried Ava, rushing over. "Are

you alright? What happened?"

"Yes. I've been wanting to faint since we stepped into this place yesterday," she said, sitting back up. "Well, at least pretend to, anyway."

Phoebe got up and raced over to the hat, mixing bowl and pasta machine. "I can't believe that they came back with us to real time. But then again, maybe I can believe it after the crazy time we just had." She sprawled on the floor. "I never thought I'd be so happy to see this cottage right now."

"I'm always happy to see this cottage. Especially now!" said Ava, hugging the corner of the rosette fireplace. "But we never really left the cottage in the first place. We only left real time, I guess."

"Well, whatever it was we left," said Phoebe, getting up, "you have to admit that this cottage is HAUNTED!"

Ava shrugged and nodded slowly. "But in a really special way. I mean, look who's been here: Captain Thunderbolt; Vanessa's great-grandfather, Mr Lui; and – making it super special – my Nonna and Nonno." A thought raced across her mind. "And you know what else,

Phoebe? They all helped make this town what it is today. Think about it: Pelusi's Pasta Piazza, Lui's Herbal and Traditional Medicine and–"

"And my favourite," blurted Phoebe. "Thunderbolt's Tavern. Those people in the next town are wrong to say Thunderbolt was never here. I can't wait to show this hat to my dad. He'll know who to show it to as proof it was Thunderbolt's. Of course, I'll say we *found* the hat in the cottage."

Ava smiled. "It's true. Just like we found proof that Vanessa's great-great-grandfather lived here. Even if it was only for one week."

She picked up the mixing stick with the name "Lui" on it. "All the more reason why the cottage shouldn't be knocked over. Phoebe, we should talk with Vanessa's parents, too, and show them what we found," Ava said.

"Yeah," said Phoebe. "I wonder how Vanessa will feel about this cottage when she finds out it was part of her family, too."

"She definitely won't want her dad to knock over the cottage for a pool," said Ava, picking up the pasta machine. "I know how my aunty and my mum are going to feel when I show them this. They'll be so excited! I'm going to plant a tomato patch while I am here on holidays, like Nonna and Nonno had, but a lot smaller. Come on, Phoebe, let's go and save this cottage. Just like that last card said."

"Hey," said Phoebe, smiling. "Which one of us won the game of cards?"

Ava looked at the two piles of cards on the floor. "Should we call it a draw? Or maybe we should play again to decide a clear winner."

Chapter 12

The Second Dare

Phoebe opened her mouth, but only a croaking sound came out. Then she bolted over, scooped the cards from the ground into their packet and put them into the box with the sand timer. "Does that answer your question? Let's call it a draw!"

Ava couldn't stop laughing. "Totally agree, Phoebe." She took the box from Phoebe and placed it back on the fireplace mantel where they'd found it last night.

"Wait, Ava, should we hide the game instead? It's a pretty scary game to play, after all," said Phoebe, as she pulled out an old, woven basket from one of the cupboards and carefully placed the pasta machine, the mixing bowl and stick, and the hat inside it.

"True," said Ava. "But, as scary as it is, there's so much to learn about the history of the cottage from it, too. Someone like Vanessa would learn heaps!"

Ava carried the basket out of the cottage, hugging it tightly, while Phoebe carried their sleeping bags and backpacks. They were halfway down the path between the cottage and the main house when Vanessa waved to them from where she was playing basketball. She raced out of her yard towards them with Hayden.

"Hi, Ava," said Hayden, when he came over with Vanessa. "Haven't seen you in ages!"

"And you nearly didn't!" said Vanessa. "This pair stayed overnight in the cottage! And survived!"

"No way!" gushed Hayden. "Really? In the haunted cottage?"

"Sure did," said Phoebe.

"Which means, Vanessa," said Ava, "that you'll talk with your parents about not knocking over the cottage?"

Vanessa nodded. "A dare is a dare. Besides, now that you guys have stayed in it, I really think that cottage will make a super-cute sleepover place for after our pool parties."

"And, just in case you have trouble convincing your parents, we'll come over and show them this," said Ava, holding up the mixing bowl and stick with the name "Lui" engraved into it.

"Hey! That's our family's name!" blurted Vanessa, showing the bowl and stick to Hayden. "Where did you find this?"

"In the cottage," said Phoebe.

"Vanessa," said Ava, "did you know your great-great-grandfather who started the family's pharmacy once lived there?"

"No way!" said Vanessa. "Mum would love to put this on display for the celebrations next week! I'm pretty sure she doesn't even know that he lived there, since the family photos were destroyed years ago."

"Your parents would know how to check that he did," said Phoebe.

"I suppose," said Vanessa, carefully stirring the stick inside the bowl. "Are there any more things in the cottage that belonged to our great-great-grandfather? I'd love to find them."

"Me too!" said Hayden.

"Maybe," said Ava, slowly, "you could go inside the cottage and have a look."

She looked at Vanessa calmly.

“Well, if you’re sure it isn’t haunted,” said Vanessa.

Ava thought for a moment. “Why don’t you and Hayden stay overnight in the cottage and see for yourselves. Go on, Vanessa, I dare you ...”